The Stranger Who Lived in a Merry-Go-Round

Ruth Silvestre

The Stranger Who Lived in a Merry-Go-Round

Illustrated by Caroline Ewan
Cover illustration by John Steven Gurney

A
LITTLE APPLE
PAPERBACK

Scholastic Inc.

New York   Toronto   London   Auckland   Sydney

No part of this publication may be reproduced in whole or in part, or stored in a retrieval system, or transmitted in any form, or by any means, electronic, mechanical, photocopying, recording, or otherwise, without written permission of the publisher. For information regarding permission, write to Hippo Books, Scholastic Publications, Ltd., 10 Earlham Street, London WC2H 9LN, England.

ISBN 0-590-45573-7

Text copyright © 1991 by Ruth Silvestre. Illustrations copyright © 1991 by Caroline Ewan. All rights reserved. Published by Scholastic Inc., 730 Broadway, New York, NY 10003, by arrangement with Hippo Books. APPLE PAPERBACKS is a registered trademark of Scholastic Inc.

12 11 10 9 8 7 6 5 4 3 2 1   3 4 5 6 7 8/9

Printed in the U.S.A.   28

First Scholastic printing, May 1993

Chapter One

It was Saturday morning and Joe was just going out. Joe always went exploring on Saturdays. His father had a restaurant called TONY'S. Joe's mother and his Aunt Nina worked there, and Saturday was their busiest day. It was Joe's day to go exploring.

Hooked to his belt Joe had a

compass, a plastic water bottle and a pouch with a coin in it. This was for the telephone in case he ever got lost. He never had. His father had shown him where his road was on the street map. Joe loved maps. He had them pinned all over his bedroom.

Joe locked the door carefully and dropped the keys through the mail-box. He walked down the steps. It was summer and the sun was warm. He sniffed the air. It smelled good. Next door's tree was covered in white flowers. The branches hung over the pavement. As he walked underneath Joe looked up and took a big sniff. Wow! They smelled as strong as Aunt Nina's perfume. He felt the whole world

was a little bit crazy today. It was just the day for an adventure.

He waited for the green light so that he could cross the road safely, then he strolled on. He jumped on all the low walls, balancing along them with his arms out, like an airplane. In the gutter he found an old tin can. He kicked it in front of him all along the pavement. It made a wonderful din — bingle, bangle, bong! He stroked a cat that was lying on the wall. Its fur was warm from the sun and it rolled over and purred like an engine.

Joe walked on and on. He felt bursting with energy. He looked at everything. How interesting the world was. When he was grown up he would explore every bit of it. He turned another corner and suddenly realized he'd never been down this road before. Good, he thought, now I'm really exploring.

There were houses on one side of the road and a high hedge on the other. It was full of spiders' webs. Joe picked a long piece of grass and poked it gently into the edge of a web. He shook the web and waited. A fat spider came dashing out to see if he'd caught a fly.

Joe laughed. "Got you that time!" he said.

The houses stopped and the road grew narrower. It was a bit muddy and seemed to be coming to an end. But Joe could see a path. He pushed his way through the tall weeds. He stomped down the stinging nettles and smelled their bitter smell. The path climbed a slope and halfway up Joe stopped. In the distance, through the bushes, he could see something. It was large and round and had many colors. Joe was amazed. For a moment he stood quite still. Then he began to run, pushing his way through. He could hardly believe his eyes.

"A merry-go-round," he whispered. "It's a merry-go-round."

He looked at the animals with their twisting brass poles. There was no mistake. It was a real, old, merry-go-round. But what was it doing there? There were weeds and grass growing all round it and it looked a bit lopsided too. It must have been there for years and years, thought Joe. He went slowly towards it. He was very excited. In all his exploring he had never discovered anything like this. He went closer until he could look up at one of the great animals. It was a horse, black with staring eyes. The one behind it was white with spots and the next one looked as though it might have been a zebra but the stripes were almost worn away.

Next to the spotted horse was a

big bird. Joe supposed it was an os-trich. Then he saw a giraffe and a dragon which was so long that there were three seats on its back. Each animal had a twisting golden pole through the middle which fixed it to the floor and to the painted top. All around the edge of the roof were faded letters. It was hard to read them because the paint was peeling off.

Joe began to walk around.

ANIMAL GALLOPERS

"Animal what?" said Joe aloud. He was just about to start around again when a door in the middle of the merry-go-round flew open and a head popped out.

Chapter Two

Joe stood quite still. He stared into the blackest yet brightest eyes that he had ever seen. The head came farther out and he could see the whole person. It was a very small, very old woman. She was all wrapped in brown like a faded leaf. She wore boots with the tops rolled over and on her head she had a man's cap. This almost made Joe laugh but there was something about this old woman that stopped him. She slipped between the animals and stepped down, peering at him closely.

"And who are you?" she asked. Her voice was thin but sharp.

Joe looked at her. "I'm not supposed to talk to strangers," he said.

"Please yourself," she answered. Then, "Quite right!"

They looked at one another.

She can't be very dangerous, thought Joe. She's really old and she's not much bigger than I am. He wondered if he ought to shake hands and decided that he'd better.

"I'm Joe," he said as he held out his hand. The old woman smiled. She had a tooth missing at the front just like Joe had when he first started school. But he'd grown a new one a long time ago.

The smile made the old woman's brown face go into lots of creases and her black eyes almost disappeared. She took Joe's hand in hers and shook it gently. Then she turned it over and looked into his palm.

"You'll have a long life, my dear," she said softly. "A long life. See, there it is. In your hand." With her brown finger she traced a line across his palm and down to his wrist. It tickled. She looked up at him. "And what's more, my dear," she said, "you're going to do a lot of traveling, yes, a lot of traveling."

Joe was pleased. She was smart to know that, this funny old woman.

"That's because I'm going to be an explorer," he said. "I'm going all over the world."

"I see." She nodded. She still held his hand and looked at him with those black eyes. "Maybe you will," she said, "maybe you will."

Her hand was very small and dry as paper. Joe pulled his own hand away gently. "Is this your merry-go-round?" he asked. "What's it doing here?"

"What's it doing here?" repeated the old woman. "It's not doing anything. It's like me, too old to work and too tired to go traveling. It's my home. I live in it and," she waved her arm, "I have all my friends around me. What could be better than that, eh?"

"Nothing," said Joe. He didn't know what else to say.

She climbed back onto the merry-go-round and Joe followed. "This is Duke," she said, patting the spotted horse, "and this is George, the giraffe." She laughed a little wheezy laugh. "He's got such a long neck he easily gets a sore throat. I have to remember to put his scarf on when the weather gets cold." She turned suddenly and looked at Joe with her head on one side. She's crazy thought Joe, nice but crazy.

"Would you like a cup of tea?" she asked him.

"Er — yes, please." Joe didn't really like tea but it seemed the only thing to say.

"This way, then." The old woman stepped between the animals and disappeared through the narrow doorway into the middle of the merry-go-round. Joe followed.

He found himself in the most amazing home that he had ever seen. To begin with, it was, as you might expect, round. In the middle was all the machinery which worked the merry-go-round, with something hanging on every knob and handle. There were bags and baskets, saucepans and bits of cloth. Joe saw a knife and fork on a string,

a dusty mirror, a pair of slippers and some big, black scissors. In every space between the wheels and cogs were papers and old letters. Above his head were lines with more things hanging from them. Every part of this strange, round room was crammed full.

The old woman filled a kettle from a jug and put a flame to a tiny stove. "Now, let me see," she said, "what about a cookie? Boys like cookies." She took down a tin.

"Yes. Yes, please," murmured Joe, still gazing around this strangest of strange homes. He walked slowly round the machinery until he came back to where the old woman was pouring the water into a teapot. "You haven't got a bed," he said.

"Quite right," she answered, unhooking two cups from the wall.

Joe was puzzled. "But where do you sleep then?"

She chuckled. "Bless me, why, in my comfy old chair, of course. When you get to be as old as me you don't need so much sleep." She looked at Joe. "I'm not growing like you are, you know. It's more like I'm shrinking." She laughed. "And anyway," she went on, "it is a pity to waste all the night hours. I like to watch the moon and the stars, and when it's not too cold I wait for my night friends."

"Your night friends?" Joe did not understand.

"Porcupines, they're my night friends. Hotchiwitchis we used to call them when I was a girl."

Joe laughed. "Hotchiwitchis!" he said. "That's a funny word."

"It's a gypsy name," said the old woman. "It's not English."

"I know some Italian words," said Joe. "My grandmother is Italian. So's my dad and my Aunt Nina. My grandmother's gone back to Italy," he added sadly. "She used to live with us but the cold in New England got into her bones, so she went back."

"My bones are used to the cold," said the old woman, pouring the tea into cups. They took them outside and sat down on the edge of the merry-go-round in the sun. Joe munched his cookie.

"Yes," said the old woman, pointing. "Under these bricks, that's
where they've got their nest, my
porcupines. See that little space?
That's where they come strolling
out, snuffling along to see what
they can find. They just enjoy a
drop of bread and milk." She

smiled. "And sometimes I get another visitor."

"Who?" asked Joe.

"The old fox," she answered. "He likes eggs. He'll come right up and take one from my hand. So, you see, it wouldn't do to be fast asleep when my visitors come, would it now?"

"No," said Joe. He looked at her. She was a strange old woman but he liked her. "Have you always lived here in the merry-go-round?" he asked.

"Oh, no," she laughed and hugged her knees. "Why, when I was your age — how old are you?"

"Seven and three quarters," said Joe, "nearly eight."

"Very nice," she said. "Well — I

lived in a wagon then with my two brothers. Travelers we were. Always going somewhere different."

"That sounds great," said Joe. "Like exploring, really."

"I suppose it was." The old woman smiled. "We made clothes pegs and come springtime we'd pick flowers and tie them in bunches to sell."

"Didn't you go to school, then?" asked Joe.

She grinned at him. "Once or twice, when we stayed somewhere for a few weeks."

"Gosh!" said Joe. "I have to go every day — except weekends, of course, and holidays."

"Things were different in them days," said the old woman. "We didn't go to school much but we learned a lot of other things. We were always busy, and when we ran home the fire would be crackling and my mother would have something good cooking in a big pot." She sighed, smiling to herself. She stopped talking and closed her eyes. Joe hoped she wasn't going to fall asleep.

"And the merry-go-round?" he asked. "What about the merry-go-round?"

The old woman opened her eyes and looked at him as though she had forgotten he was there.

"Oh, the merry-go-round," she said, "that belonged to my husband. He died a long, long time ago. Every summer we'd take it all over the country. Hundreds of children riding the animals." She smiled. "Then, when it got too cold, we'd find somewhere to rest up, like here." She nodded. "Then when spring came around we'd paint it up — and off we'd go again."

"That sounds great," said Joe.

"Yes, it was." The old woman smiled at him. Then she got up and patted the spotted horse. "But we're too old now, aren't we, Duke? We stay here and look after each other." She turned suddenly. "I'm tired now. I'm off for a nap. What did you say your name was?"

"Joe," he called, watching her slide through the narrow door into the merry-go-round. "What's yours?"

"Granny Peg, they call me," she said, and the door closed.

Joe walked home thinking about Granny Peg and her merry-go-round. How wonderful it would be to go exploring all summer. On and on, somewhere new every day. That would make him happy.

He walked until he came to his dad's restaurant. He pushed the door open. It smelled good and, as usual, was very busy. "Good Italian food. Sensible prices. They always come back." That's what his dad said. Joe's mother came out of the kitchen carrying lots of plates all up her arm. She was very good at that. She smiled at him.

"Hello, Joe. Go and have your dinner. You're a bit late today."

"I've been exploring," said Joe. "I've found the most fantastic . . ."

"Yes, yes, later, Joe." His mother put down the plates and hurried to the next table with her pad and pencil on a string. She began to write down the orders.

Joe sighed and went through to the kitchen where his Aunt Nina was washing up. She dried her hands on her apron and served him a big bowl of spaghetti with loads of sauce. He didn't even bother to tell her or his father about his adventure. His father was so busy, chopping, then stirring and the fan in the kitchen made such a lot of noise that he probably wouldn't hear him anyway. His father grinned at him over a cloud of steam.

"You OK, Joe?" he shouted.

"OK," called Joe. He curled the spaghetti around his fork and slid it into his mouth. He was really hungry. He began to wonder if it had all been a dream. An old woman living in a merry-go-round? Who would believe that?

Chapter Three

On Sundays the restaurant was closed. Joe's father always stayed in bed late and Joe's mother cooked the dinner. When his grandmother had lived with them she had always cooked on Sundays.

Joe wished she hadn't gone back to Italy. She had always had time to talk to him. He could have told her about the old woman in the merry-go-round. When she started to get pains in her back and her legs the doctor said she needed the sun. So she went back to Italy. Now all Joe got were postcards. He had them all pinned up under his maps. It looked nice in Italy. He wished they could go there but his dad said they would have to wait until the restaurant was making more money.

After they had all had their dinner, it was Joe's mother's turn for a rest. She took off her apron, hung it on the back of the kitchen door and said, "That's it!" She put her feet up on the sofa and began to watch the television. Joe knew that in ten minutes she would be fast asleep.

Joe got out the street map of his town. He opened it on the floor. First he found his own road. Then he tried to remember which way he had gone yesterday. How many corners had he turned? He traced it with his finger. No. That couldn't be the way. That road came out on the big, main road. He went back to his own road and began again.

"What are you doing, Joe?" his father asked.

"I'm trying to find where I went yesterday," he said.

His father came and sat on the floor beside him.

"I went down there," said Joe, pointing on the map, "across the main road — "

"At the crossing?" asked his father.

"Of course," sighed Joe. "Then I walked down that street. You see. BERRY STREET. I remember the name. Then I turned by the mailbox and then — oh no, I can't find it."

"What exactly are you looking for?" asked his father, yawning.

"A road that doesn't go anywhere really," said Joe.

"Doesn't sound very interesting to me." Joe's father stretched out on the floor and closed his eyes.

"It was! It was!" cried Joe. "It

started out as an ordinary road but then it got narrower and narrower and then there was a merry-go-round."

His father opened one eye and looked at him. "A merry-go-round?"

"Yes," said Joe.

"At the end of a road going nowhere?" His father opened his other eye.

"Yes!" cried Joe. "And there was an old woman living in the middle of the merry-go-round."

"JOE!" His father sighed. "I thought you'd grown out of all that. You remember the crocodile you saw in someone's front yard? And the time you told us you'd seen a spaceship landing?"

"I know, I know!" shouted Joe. "I was small then. Now I'm nearly eight. She's real, I tell you. I knew you wouldn't believe me. I knew it!"

Joe's father reached into his pocket. "Here," he said, "here's some money. Go get an ice cream, Joe, and calm down. I'm tired."

When Joe went to bed that night he lay thinking about his adventure. He got out of bed. There was a big, shining moon. He wondered if Granny Peg was putting out bread and milk for the porcupines. What had she called them? Hotchiwitchis, that was it. He smiled as he remembered the funny name. And the old fox! Imagine giving him an egg. He got back into bed and moved his pillow so that he could still see the moon. I will go and see her again next Saturday, he thought as he fell asleep.

Chapter Four

Next Saturday when Joe got up it was raining but by the time he had finished his breakfast it had stopped. Joe was pleased. His father had already gone to work. Saturday night was the busiest night at the restaurant.

Joe got his things ready to go exploring. As he was filling his water bottle his mother came in the back door. She had been hanging some laundry on the line. "It's going to be a fine day after all," she said. "Look, Joe, all those clouds are blowing away."

"I'm glad," said Joe. "I'm going exploring."

"Don't go too far," said his mother. "I worry about you, Joe." The phone rang and she ran to answer it. "Yes. Yes, I'm coming!" she shouted and she banged the phone down again. "Your father!" she said. "He thinks I've got ten pairs of hands. Lock up carefully, Joe."

"Yes, Mom," said Joe.

"And wear your watch," she said, putting on her coat.

"Yes, Mom."

"And come for your dinner as soon as you're hungry."

"Yes, Mom!"

She kissed him and ran out of the house.

*   *   *

Joe was a bit worried in case he couldn't find the way to the merry-go-round. Once he was across the main road and onto Berry Street he looked about him very carefully.

Yes, he was quite sure he had walked past this turning and the next one and — he stood on the corner. Was it here he had turned? Suddenly he noticed a house with a swing in the garden. Yes, he remembered that. Good. He ran on. He crossed over and hurried down the next street.

Yes. He was excited now. The road to the merry-go-round was around the next corner. There it was. The name was almost hidden in the hedge. WILLOW ROAD. Good, now he'd be able to look it up on the street map and mark it with a pen. He might show it to his dad. Crocodiles! Didn't Dad know that he'd grown up? He would be eight soon.

He raced down the road, past where the houses stopped. The spiders' webs were still full of rain drops. They sparkled in the sunshine. But Joe didn't have time for them. He ran up the sloping path, then slowed down. Yes, there it was. He could see the top of the merry-go-round clearly over the bushes. He was so glad it hadn't been a dream.

When he pushed his way through the bushes he could see Granny Peg. She had been doing some washing just like his mom.

Except that she didn't have a machine. She had a big bowl of soapy water on top of an old box, and she had already hung a few things on a line. She looked exactly the same except for a long, striped apron which came almost down to her feet.

He watched her wring out a towel and spread it on a bush to dry. She hadn't heard him coming but the moment he stepped nearer she looked up. For a minute she looked quite angry, then she smiled.

"Oh, it's you, Joe," she said. "Where have you been?"

"School," said Joe. "I told you I have to go to school."

"Right," said Granny Peg.

"Didn't you make your children go to school?" asked Joe.

Granny Peg looked sad. "I never had any children, Joe," she said.

"Then how can you be a granny?"

"I'm not a real granny. It's just what they called me — all those children who used to ride the merry-go-round."

"Oh, I see," said Joe.

"As a matter of fact, I've no one now in the whole world," she said.

"You have!" cried Joe. "You've got the porcupines and the fox."

"Of course I have." She smiled. "Cup of tea, Joe?" she asked as she poured away the washing water. Joe nodded. He didn't really want a cup of tea but he did want another look inside the merry-go-round. "You'll have to go and get some water," she said. "I've used it all up for the laundry."

"Where do I get it from?" asked Joe, looking around.

Granny Peg handed him a plastic water bottle. It was just like the one on his belt but much bigger.

"Follow that path," she said, "and you'll find the water tap."

Joe went the way she had pointed and found a pipe sticking up out of the ground with a tap on the top. When he had filled the bottle it was quite heavy and he had to carry it back slowly.

While Granny Peg boiled the kettle he had another look inside the merry-go-round.

"Whatever do you cut with this great big pair of scissors?" he asked. "They don't look very sharp."

"I bet if you were to go on guessing for a week you'd never know." Granny Peg smiled at him. "I don't use them. They belonged to my husband."

43

"Well, what did he cut, then?" asked Joe.

"Candy."

"Candy?" said Joe. "What kind of candy?"

"The best candy I ever tasted," said Granny Peg. "My husband used to make it. He would boil up a great pan of butter and sugar and spices. Then he would pull up a long strip like this. As it cooled he'd twist it and then cut it with those great scissors. I can tell you it smelled wonderful."

"Mm," said Joe, "I love candy."

"I wish I could give you a taste, Joe, but nobody makes candy like that now."

"I wish they did," said Joe. He sat down on the edge of Granny Peg's comfy chair. "Did you sleep in this chair when you were a little girl?" he asked.

"Oh, no," said Granny Peg, reaching into the cookie jar. "I had a nice bed in our wagon and my brothers, they slept in a little tent. Other kids used to shout 'Gypsy Gypsy live in a tent. Can't afford to pay the rent,' but we didn't care. We didn't want to live in a house anyway. Here's your tea."

"I will sleep in a tent when I grow up and go exploring," said Joe. He followed the old woman outside and they sat down on the edge of the merry-go-round.

It was a beautiful morning. All the clouds had gone. Birds were singing in the bushes. Joe told

Granny Peg all about his mother and father and the restaurant. He told her how busy they always were and how he wished and wished that his grandmother hadn't gone back to Italy. Granny Peg listened. She sat very still, her head on one side. Suddenly she said, quietly, so quietly that Joe wasn't sure he'd heard her, "What about a ride? Huh, Joe?"

"A ride?" said Joe slowly, looking around. "Did you say a ride?"

Granny Peg nodded. Her black eyes were very bright.

"But — " said Joe, "does it still work — this merry-go-round?"

"Only for special people," she said softly. "It all depends."

"Depends on what?"

"Whether you've got your head in the clouds or your feet on the ground." She laughed, the little rusty laugh he had heard before. Her small brown face creased up and her eyes glittered. Joe looked at her. She was crazy, quite crazy. He knew that and yet — there was something about her that he couldn't explain.

"Choose your seat!" she suddenly cried in a loud, clear voice. "CHOOSE YOUR SEAT, PLEASE!"

Joe laughed. He climbed onto the back of Duke, the spotted horse. "I'll choose this one!" he cried.

"And I'll ride the ostrich." The old woman climbed easily onto its back. She stretched out her arm.

"Hold my hand for a minute," she said, "and shut your eyes and wish and wish and wish."

Joe closed his eyes and wished. For a moment nothing happened, then, suddenly, his heart seemed to float right out of his body. He heard — faintly at first and then louder — strange, old-fashioned music. Very slowly, the old merry-go-round began to move. He felt the spotted horse rise up in the air, then slowly sink, and then rise up again. They were going around. The merry-go-round was turning and turning and turning. Faster and faster. He opened his eyes and looked at Granny Peg. She was hanging onto the golden pole with her head thrown back. Her long

gray hair was flying out behind her in the wind and she was singing in a high piping voice.

Joe began to laugh. He closed his eyes again. The merry-go-round went faster and suddenly Duke seemed to come alive beneath him. He felt its warmth and smelled its smell. It tossed its head and neighed with delight. "Faster! Faster!" yelled Joe. And round and round they went. He felt as if they were soaring over the whole world. He felt as if he would burst with joy. What an adventure! What a ride!

At last, after what seemed like forever, and yet no time at all, they began to slow down. Slower and slower they went. Joe felt his horse grow hard and wooden again. The music faded. They stopped. Joe opened his eyes. There were the trees and bushes and the laundry out to dry. The birds were still singing and the sun still shining high in the sky. Joe looked at Granny Peg, very small and very still beside him on her scratched and peeling ostrich.

"Did it really happen?" he asked after a moment. "Did we really go round and round and did the animals . . . ?"

The old woman leaned towards him and put a papery finger on his lips. "Ssh," she said softly. "You mustn't talk about it. It's a secret. It won't work for just anyone."

She climbed slowly down from

the ostrich's back and rubbed her hands on her apron, yawning. "Now I'm really tired," she said, smiling at Joe. "I'm ready for forty winks in my comfy old chair. But you must come another day." She waved her hand and disappeared into the merry-go-round. The door banged shut behind her.

Joe was alone. He slid off the spotted horse. He walked slowly down the steps. He looked back at the merry-go-round. He saw the weeds growing up through the floor. It couldn't have gone around. It was impossible and yet — it had. Joe knew something very strange had happened. This must be a magic place, he thought.

He ran all the way back to the restaurant but by the time he got there, he knew he was not going to try telling anyone about anything. As he lay in bed that night, he thought over and over again about the wonderful ride and his dreams were filled with old-fashioned music and galloping horses.

Chapter Five

The next Friday as he walked home from school, Joe was thinking about the merry-go-round. He would go tomorrow. He wondered if he would get another ride. He hoped so. Then he would really believe it had happened.

There were only three more days of school left before summer vacation began. It was very hot and Joe was thirsty, so he walked round the corner to the restaurant. It was quiet; there were only two customers eating ice cream. His father was reading a newspaper. He got

Joe some very cold orange juice from the kitchen.

"Where's Mom?" asked Joe.

His father looked gloomy. "She's looking after your Aunt Nina," he said.

"Why? What's the matter with her?" asked Joe.

"She feels bad," said his father, "and the doctor says she must stay in bed for at least three days. I don't know how we're going to manage without her."

Joe could see that his father was really worried.

"What about me?" he asked. "I can help you, can't I?"

His father looked at him. "I suppose you could do a bit." He smiled at Joe. "Yes. Why not?"

Joe was pleased that his father needed him. I can go to the merry-go-round another day. In the summer I can go any day I like, he thought.

Joe's mother stuck her head in the door. "I'm going to the drug store to get some medicine," she called. "I'll be back soon."

"I'm going to help you in the restaurant. Dad says I can," said Joe, proudly.

His mother looked at him and smiled. "Good boy," she said. "You'd better start by giving us a hand this evening."

Joe had sometimes helped in the restaurant before but only for fun. This time he felt really important. After he had eaten his own supper, Joe's father tied an apron around Joe's waist and gave him a pad and a pencil just like his mother's. His mom showed him how to write down the orders quickly. RAV for ravioli, SP for spaghetti, CH for chicken. Joe soon got the hang of it. He enjoyed it. The customers all smiled at him and they didn't seem

to mind waiting just a bit longer
than usual. At first his mother
checked every order but when she
saw that he could manage she left
him on his own and dashed back
and forth into the kitchen.

When they paid the bill, the customers left him money. At the end
of the evening, Joe had collected

nearly ten dollars. "Gosh!" he said. "I think I'll do this more often. I can save up to go to Italy."

"Oh, no, you won't. You're too young," said his father. "It's not allowed. This is just an emergency."

But he put his arm around Joe and hugged him and Joe felt happy. His legs ached and he was very tired. It was past eleven o'clock when he and his mother walked home.

"What time do we start tomorrow?" yawned Joe, as he pulled on his pajamas.

"Ten o'clock," said his mother, "so you'd better go straight off to sleep."

Saturday was a really busy day. All morning Joe rushed around with plates. Everyone seemed to be in a hurry. In the afternoon he fell asleep in a chair. The evening was the busiest time of all. On Sunday he understood why his father and mother were always so tired. Joe fell asleep in front of the television just like his mother.

Aunt Nina had the flu. She stayed in bed all that week. But on Saturday she was better and Joe did not need to help in the restaurant. He was glad to have a day off. He would go exploring and see Granny Peg again.

He was quite sure of the way now. He raced along Willow Road, past the spiders' webs, through the bushes until he reached the merry-go-round.

There was no sign of Granny Peg. It was very quiet. Joe walked around the merry-go-round. Then he walked around again, whistling loudly. He hoped she would come out. He climbed the steps and stood outside the narrow door. He knocked. He waited. He knocked again. He felt sure she was in there.

"Granny Peg!" he shouted. "It's me. Joe."

He thought he heard a sound. It could have been a cough. He called again. Why wouldn't she come out? He waited, looking at the door, but it never opened.

Joe felt very sad. Why wouldn't she open the door? He walked down the steps. He went down the path to the water tap and looked back. There was no sign of her. Oh well, he thought, if she won't come out, she won't. I suppose I might as well go on exploring.

He walked on down the path. At first it was very quiet, but as he went farther he began to hear the noise of cars and buses. At last he came to a high fence, as high as a house. It had a small door cut into it.

Joe opened the door, stepped through and was surprised to find himself on a busy street. On the other side of the road were shops. I suppose this is where Granny Peg goes shopping, he thought. He crossed the road carefully and looked back at the high fence. It had posters stuck all over it. You could hardly see the door. No one would notice it, not unless they were looking for it.

He crossed back again and slipped through the door. I'll just have one more try at the merry-go-round, he said to himself. She might have been asleep in her old chair. But when he knocked and called there was still no reply.

Joe walked home sadly. What if Granny Peg were ill? Perhaps she had the flu like his Aunt Nina. His dad said there was a lot of flu going around. And Granny Peg had no one in the world. She had told him so. He thought he'd heard her cough. Who would go to get her medicine?

When Joe lay in bed that night he couldn't sleep. He was really worried. He wanted to tell his mom and dad but he knew they wouldn't believe him.

Chapter Six

On Sunday afternoon Joe's father was reading the paper when he suddenly looked up. "Hey, Joe," he called. "It seems I was wrong."

"What about?" asked Joe.

"Your old merry-go-round," said his father. "Look, there's a picture of it in the paper."

Joe rushed to see. Sure enough,

there was the merry-go-round among the trees and bushes. There was even a picture of Granny Peg as well.

"What does it say?" begged Joe, who could see that there were lots of long words. "Re-de-vel-op-ment." He spelled it out. "What does that mean?"

"It means," said his father, "that the City Council has bought that land and they're going to build there."

"But what about the merry-go-round and Granny Peg?" cried Joe.

Joe's father read a bit more. "It says here," he said, "that the City has offered Miss Peg a place in a home for old people on the other side of town but she doesn't want to move."

"Of course she doesn't!" shouted Joe. "She belongs in the merry-go-round. And what about all her friends?"

"What friends?" asked his father.

Joe told him about the porcupines and the fox. He didn't tell him about Duke the spotted horse, or George the giraffe, or the ride. Especially not the ride. He couldn't explain everything.

"It says here," said his father gently, "that Miss Peg is eighty-four years old. That's very old, Joe. Much older than your grandmother in Italy. Perhaps she would be better off in a nice warm home. It must be cold living in a merry-go-round. Old people need someone to look after them, you know."

"She's used to the cold. She told me so," said Joe. Then he remembered. "Oh, Dad," he said, "when I went to see her yesterday she wouldn't come out. I think she might have the flu like Aunt Nina."

Joe looked so worried that his father folded up his paper and grabbed his jacket. "Come on, Joe," he said. "You take me. You show me your merry-go-round and we'll go see the old lady. How's that?"

Joe was very pleased. His father never went out on Sundays, as a rule. Joe hopped along beside him, pointing out the way.

Soon they came to the merry-go-round. Joe's father stood still for a moment and looked at it. "Just think how many children must have had a ride on that," he said softly.

Joe looked at his father. "Granny Peg can make magic, Dad."

"Can she?" His father smiled at him. "Well — there's not a lot of that around these days, I can tell you."

They walked up to the merry-go-round, hand in hand. Joe saw that the door was open just a crack.

"Granny Peg," he called, "it's Joe. Please come out. I've brought my dad to see you." There was no reply. "Granny Peg," Joe called again, "have you got the flu?"

The door opened wider and

there she was. She stood in the doorway looking at them both with her bright, black eyes. "No, I haven't got the flu," she said. "I'm just not up to much."

She came out slowly and stood on the steps of the merry-go-round.

"I thought you were some more of those folks from the City Council poking around," she said. "They make me sick. Always talking nonsense." She patted the tail of the spotted horse. "We're not going nowhere, Duke, are we?" she said.

Joe looked at his father.

"Hello, Miss Peg," said Joe's father. "I'm Tony from the restaurant. I'm Joe's father. We read in the paper about the City buying the land. Didn't they write and tell you about it?"

Granny Peg looked at him. She went into the merry-go-round and came back with a tin box full of letters. She handed them to Joe's father. "You have a look," she said.

Joe's father took the letters. "But you haven't opened them," he said.

"What use would that be," said Granny Peg, "seeing as how I can't read them?"

"You need some glasses," said Joe.

Granny Peg shook her head. "My eyes are as sharp as they ever were," she said. "I just never learned to read."

"Why not?" asked Joe.

"I suppose I was never in school long enough," she said.

Joe's father was looking through the letters. "I'm afraid you should have gotten someone to read these for you," he said. "It looks to me as though the City has bought this land and you will have to move."

"Well, I won't!" said Granny Peg sharply. "This is my home and I'm staying here." She got up stiffly. "You can take the letters if you like. They're no use to me. Now I'm tired. I'm off for my forty winks." She did look tired and very small, thought Joe.

"I'll send Joe around with some food for you tomorrow," said his father. "Some of my soup. That will cheer you up, huh?"

"Please yourself," she said and closed the door.

Chapter Seven

The next day and the day after, and all that week, Joe took Granny Peg food from the restaurant. One day it was soup, another day a nice piece of chicken, another day a pizza. She really didn't like the pizza. Each day they talked but Joe could see that Granny Peg was unhappy.

When he went on Friday she was very angry. She was banging a broom, sweeping down her steps.

"I told her," she shouted, when she saw Joe.

"Told who?" he asked.

"That young woman!" she cried. "I told her — get off my steps and never come back again. I've had hundreds of children on this merry-go-round, hundreds. But I don't want you putting your foot on it, I told her."

"Who was she?" asked Joe.

"Some busybody from the City Council," said Granny Peg. "Telling me she'd found me another home. 'Now, Miss Peg,' she said. 'It's a very nice, comfortable home,' she said. 'You'll like it,' she said. How does she know what I'd like?" Granny Peg glared at Joe. "She never had her head in the clouds, never!" She looked at Joe for a moment. "Not like you and me, Joe, huh?" she said softly. She smiled at him. Her old black eyes shone.

She didn't need to speak another word. Joe knew. Together they climbed up onto the merry-go-round. Together they closed their eyes and the magic began. First the music, very faint but getting clearer. Then the moving, slowly, oh so slowly at first. Just one turn and then another. Then faster and faster. Joe felt again the rush of the wind on his face. He heard the neighing of his horse and he was filled with a wild happiness.

Joe and Granny Peg held hands and he heard her singing. He wished it could go on forever but he knew it couldn't. Sure enough, they began to slow down, down, down. The music faded away and they were still. Joe opened his eyes.

Granny Peg was looking at him. "That was what I needed," she said. "Just one more ride on the merry-go-round." She climbed down. She patted the horse. "Dear old Duke," she said, "you're my good old friend." They went into the merry-go-round.

"Shall I make you a cup of tea?" asked Joe.

Granny Peg shook her head. "No, no thank you, Joe," she said. "I'm tired. You know, Joe, I've had such a good, long life. I've done all my exploring now, but you, you've got all yours to do. Don't you forget that, Joe, will you?" She smiled at him. "Goodbye, Joe," she said. "Close the door after you."

The next day, Joe was too busy to go to the merry-go-round. Some friends of his father's had booked the whole restaurant for a party. Joe had to help his father put up extra tables and tie balloons and paper chains across the ceiling.

"Whose birthday is it?" asked Joe.

"Nobody's," said his father. "It's an engagement party — when somebody decides to get married."

"I'm never going to get married," said Joe. "I'm going to be an explorer."

"Perhaps you might marry another explorer," said his mother.

"Girls can't be explorers, can they?" asked Joe.

"Of course they can," said his

mother. "If they don't have to work all day in a restaurant, that is." Joe's father laughed.

It was a great party. Everyone sang and danced and had fun. Joe was allowed to stay up until the end. He thought that getting married couldn't be too bad. Everyone had been so happy.

He was so tired he slept until after eleven. Gosh! he thought when he looked at his clock, it's nearly afternoon. I've nearly missed this morning.

He went downstairs. His mother and father had gone a long time ago. Joe sat drinking orange juice and yawning. He washed himself very slowly and pulled on his jeans and his T-shirt. Then he went to the restaurant to see what his father would give him to take to Granny Peg.

Joe left the restaurant with some slices of turkey and a big piece of cake left over from the party. He walked slowly. He was still tired. It was a cloudy morning and looked as though it might rain. As he pushed his way through the bushes by the merry-go-round, Joe heard voices. He ran towards them. If it was someone else from the City Council, Granny Peg would get angry. He'd better hurry.

There was a man on the steps of the merry-go-round and another walking away towards the water tap. The door was open. The man on the steps turned and Joe saw that he was a policeman.

"Hello, sonny." He smiled at Joe.

"Where's Granny Peg?" asked Joe.

"I'm afraid — " said the policeman, then stopped. "Was she your granny?" he asked.

"No, she's my friend," said Joe.

"I've brought her her dinner. Look." He showed the policeman the package.

The policeman looked sad. "I'm afraid she won't be needing any dinner," he said softly. "What's your name?"

"Joe," whispered Joe.

"Well, Joe." The policeman closed the door into the merry-go-round and came down the steps. He put his hand on Joe's shoulder.

"Miss Peg died in her sleep," he said. "She just went to sleep and never woke up again."

Joe felt a cold, hard lump of sadness fix itself inside his chest. He knew people died. He knew nobody lived forever. He was nearly eight years old and he knew that. He just couldn't believe that he would never see Granny Peg again. He looked at the package of food and his eyes filled with tears. He didn't want the policeman to see him cry. He threw the food into the bushes and ran back the way he had come.

He sat down on the bank by the spider's web until he had finished crying. Then he wiped his eyes and blew his nose and walked back to the restaurant. But as soon as he saw his dad his eyes filled up with tears again.

When he told his mother and father what had happened they sat him down in the kitchen. "Now, you just eat this and you listen to me," said his father, putting out a big bowl of spaghetti with Joe's favorite sauce. "Of course you are sad. But you are sad for your-self. You mustn't be sad for Granny Peg. She was very old and very tired."

Joe's mother put her arm around him. "And remember, Joe," she said, "Granny Peg didn't want to move. She wanted to stay in the merry-go-round for the rest of her life, didn't she?"

Joe nodded. "But I just didn't know she had such a little bit of life left," he said. The sad feeling in his chest was still there but it wasn't as bad as before. He felt very tired.

Chapter Eight

On Monday morning a letter plopped through the letter box.

Joe picked it up. "It's from Italy!" he said. He recognized the stamp and his grandmother's writing.

His father sat down to read it and smiled. "Well, well, Joe," he said. "You're in luck. Your grandmother's won some money and she wants to buy you a plane ticket to go and see her this summer. How about that?"

Joe's eyes opened wide. "All by myself?" he said.

"Why not?" asked his father. "It will be an adventure. It'll be like exploring, won't it?"

Joe thought about it. Somehow he didn't quite feel like exploring at the moment. He still felt very sad. But he would like to see his real grandmother again.

"You'll have a good time," said his mother. "You'll be able to go to the beach with your cousins and you'll learn some more Italian, too."

Joe already knew a few words. His grandmother had talked to him often in Italian but he had forgotten lots of it.

"How many cousins have I got?" he asked.

"Three," said his father. "We'll go to buy the ticket as soon as we can. You'll have a wonderful vacation. I wish I was going."

Joe began to cheer up.

By the time the day came to go to Italy, he was very excited. His father took him to the airport. There were three other children traveling alone on the same plane. Joe sat with them and waved to his father.

When the plane took off, for a

moment it reminded him of the merry-go-round. He felt the sadness again but then he looked down and saw the fields beneath him and soon he saw the edge of the land and the beginning of the sea. It was like looking at a giant map and Joe loved maps.

Joe's grandmother was at the airport to meet him and so were his uncle and his three cousins. Carlo was ten, Elena was seven and little Marco was four. They all talked at once as they carried his bags to the car. It was very hot and sunny in Italy.

They all lived together in a house not far from the sea. Every day they went to the beach. Joe was very happy. There were so many new things to see.

His grandmother was so pleased to see him. She cooked him mountains of spaghetti and she was always giving him peaches and grapes to eat. Every evening after supper they would go for a walk into the town and eat wonderful ice cream. Joe found that he remembered lots of Italian words.

His grandmother was brown
from the sun and her legs were better. She asked him all about his father and mother and how the
restaurant was doing.

Joe was going to tell her about
Granny Peg but he didn't. He was
having such a great time he didn't

want to remember how sad he had been. He went exploring with Carlo and Elena. "When we're grown up we're going exploring all over the world together," he told his grandmother.

Soon the vacation was over. The whole family came to the airport to see him off. His cousins promised to write. Carlo was going to start learning English when he went back to school. "Next time you come you must bring your father and mother and your Aunt Nina," said his grandmother. She loaded him up with bags of special cakes she had made for his father. She waved and waved until the plane took off and Joe flew back home.

Joe's mother and father met him at the airport. They hugged and kissed him and his father was very pleased when he saw the special cakes. "My favorites!" he cried.

"You've grown, Joe," said his mother, "and look how brown you are. Did you have a good time?"

"Great!" said Joe. "Can I go again next year?"

"We'll see," said his mother.

For the next few days Joe felt very tired. "You always feel like that after a vacation," said his father. "Cheer up. You'll be going back to school next week."

On the last day of vacation Joe's mother took him to buy some new clothes. They went by bus and after they had finished shopping they had lunch in a restaurant. His mother enjoyed that. "It makes a change for me to be waited on," she said. Joe was feeling pleased because he had new shoes, a new jacket and two new sweaters.

"It must have been all the food that Grandma gave me that made me grow out of my clothes," he said.

On the way home, Joe was looking out of the bus window when he suddenly recognized the road they were on. There was the high fence covered with posters. The bus slowed down just by the little door. He saw a man coming through it wearing a yellow hard hat. Over the top of the fence he could see a crane moving and the top of a bulldozer.

Joe slid right down in his seat. He didn't want to look. There was just a little piece of sadness still inside him somewhere.

On Monday he started in the third grade. He felt very grown up. Joe's new teacher was called Mr. Cole. Joe knew right away that he was going to like him. As soon as Joe walked into the classroom, he was quite sure.

All the walls were covered with maps and pictures of interesting places. There were pictures of Eskimos fishing through holes in the ice. There were people growing bananas and pineapples. There were mountains and rivers with crocodiles.

Mr. Cole had a cupboard with glass doors which was filled with the strangest things. He even had an ostrich egg. The biggest egg Joe had ever seen. Joe was very happy in his new class and the weeks flew by.

Chapter Nine

One day when Joe came home from school, his father was looking very worried. "We've got to look for another restaurant," he said.

"Why?" asked Joe. "What's wrong with this one?"

"It's being sold," said his father. "I'd really like some place bigger but I'm not sure if I can find one anywhere." He scratched his head and sighed. "Just when we're so busy," he said.

For the next few weeks Joe's father was always rushing off to look at places, but one day he came back looking much more cheerful.

"You've found somewhere?" asked Joe.

His father nodded. "We'll be moving the week before Christmas," he said. "It's brand new, not quite finished yet."

"Is it far away?" asked Joe.

"Not too far," said his father. "It's bigger than here. We can have four or five more tables and you should see the kitchen. Things are looking up, Joe."

Joe was pleased. "If we make a lot of money, can we all go to Italy next year?" he asked. His father laughed. "I'm not promising."

Joe was looking forward to Christmas. His father was going to buy him a bicycle. When the time for moving came, all Joe's father's friends came to help him. Joe wanted to help, too, but his parents wouldn't let him. "No, Joe," they said, "we want it to be a surprise. Wait until it's all ready."

Joe could see that they were both very excited about the new place.

On the last day before vacation, his father picked him up from school.

"Today," he said, "you're going to have your dinner in the best place in town." His eyes were shining. Joe was excited. At last he was going to see the new restaurant.

They drove through the streets. It was almost dark. People were hurrying home with their Christmas presents. Joe's father turned and stopped the car outside the back of a new building. It was cold and Joe shivered as he got out of the warm car.

They went through the back door and down a passage. Joe's father opened the door into the kitchen. His mom was there and so was his Aunt Nina. Everything was gleaming new and it was twice as big as the old kitchen.

"Wow! Fantastic!" said Joe. "You'll be able to cook piles of food in here. Gosh, I'm starving." He sat down in the brand new kitchen and started on a piece of chocolate cake.

Suddenly he stopped eating. A strange feeling came over him. He thought he could hear music. It was special, old-fashioned music. He had heard that music before. But it couldn't be. He looked at his father. He didn't know what to say.

His father smiled. "Come on, Joe," he said. "You haven't seen the rest of the restaurant."

As Joe followed his father through the door, the music got louder. He walked between the new tables with their red cloths as if he was in a dream. He could see something wonderful outside the window of his dad's new restaurant. Something round and many-colored with twisting golden poles.

"It's a merry-go-round!" he shouted. "It's Granny Peg's merry-go-round!"

Joe's father took him outside to

meet the man who had bought the merry-go-round. He told Joe how he loved old merry-go-rounds. He showed him that he had repainted every inch. Duke had bright new spots. George the giraffe looked beautiful. The whole merry-go-round gleamed and sparkled. The machinery was cleaned and oiled. Joe watched the wheels and cogs all turning.

"This new shopping center is called the Merry-Go-Round Center," said his father. "It was built on the land where Granny Peg used to live."

Joe watched the children riding the merry-go-round. They hung onto the animals and laughed and waved. He knew that they would never have a ride as wonderful as those he'd had with Granny Peg. But he looked at their happy faces and knew that she would have been very glad.

He would never forget her, the old woman who lived in the merry-go-round. He remembered what she had said the last time he saw her. "You've got all your exploring to do, Joe," she had said and she was right. As he listened to the music and watched the merry-go-round turning, Joe felt the last little corner of sadness in his heart melt away.

"Come on, Joe," said his father. "Let's switch on the lights in our new restaurant and wait for the first customers."